PUFFIN BOOKS

The PERFECT HAMBURGER

Alexander McCall Smith lives in Scotland. He is the author of more than fifty books for children and adults, including the bestselling *The No 1 Ladies Detective Agency*. In 2004 he became the winner of three Author of the Year awards. He is married with two daughters and his hobbies include playing brass and other wind instruments.

The PERFECT HAMBURGER

Alexander Mccall Smith
Illustrated by Laszlo Acs

PUFFIN

PUFFIN BOOKS

Published by the Penguin Group
Penguin Books Ltd, 80 Strand, London WC2R 0RL, England
Penguin Group (USA), Inc., 375 Hudson Street, New York, New York 10014, USA
Penguin Books Australia Ltd, 250 Camberwell Road, Camberwell, Victoria 3124, Australia
Penguin Books Canada Ltd, 10 Alcorn Avenue, Toronto, Ontario, Canada M4V 3B2
Penguin Books India (P) Ltd, 11 Community Centre, Panchsheel Park, New Delhi – 110 017, India
Penguin Group (NZ), cnr Airborne and Rosedale Roads, Albany, Auckland 1310, New Zealand
Penguin Books (South Africa) (Pty) Ltd, 24 Sturdee Avenue, Rosebank 2196, South Africa

Penguin Books Ltd, Registered Offices: 80 Strand, London WC2R 0RL, England

www.penguin.com

First published by Hamish Hamilton 1982
Published in Puffin Books 1994

032

Text copyright © Alexander McCall Smith, 1982
Illustrations copyright © Hamish Hamilton, 1982
All rights reserved

Set in Baskerville
Made and printed in England by Clays Ltd, St Ives plc

British Library Cataloguing in Publication Data
A CIP catalogue record for this book is available from the British Library

ISBN 0–140–31670–1

ISBN-13: 978–0–14–031670–4

www.greenpenguin.co.uk

MIX
Paper from
responsible sources
FSC
www.fsc.org   FSC™ C018179

Penguin Books is committed to a sustainable
future for our business, our readers and our planet.
This book is made from Forest Stewardship
Council™ certified paper.

Chapter 1

JOE LIKED HAMBURGERS. He liked hamburgers that were crisp and delicious and that had one ring of onion on the top and one on the bottom. He liked hamburgers that had just a touch of ketchup and that were big enough to sink your teeth into, even if you finished up with a stream of juice running down to the end of your chin. In fact, Joe liked most sorts of hamburger.

In the town where he lived there was only one hamburger place. This was because it was not a big town and nobody thought there would ever be room for another one. This place was run by an old man called

Mr Borthwick, who had been running it for as long as anyone could remember.

Although everybody liked Mr Borthwick, the truth of the matter was that his hamburger place was not as good as it used to be. Mr Borthwick had none of the fancy equipment that bigger hamburger places have, so his hamburgers took longer to make and were not as crisp as they should be. Also, it was plain to see that Mr Borthwick's place needed new stools, as the old ones looked very tatty indeed. A coat of paint would have transformed the place.

Joe knew there was a problem at Mr Borthwick's. Fewer and fewer people were buying hamburgers there. Those who did often complained.

"I don't know what's happened to the place," somebody would say. "It used to be so good, but now . . ."

"You're right," somebody else would add. "I had a hamburger there the other day and it was cold by the time it got to me."

Hearing this sort of thing made Joe feel worried. He was fond of Mr Borthwick and didn't like to think of his hamburger business going downhill. Yet if Mr Borthwick didn't do something to improve things then, before too long, he would have no customers left. And if somebody else chose to open up another hamburger place in competition with Mr Borthwick's, well, the old man wouldn't stand a chance.

And that's exactly what happened. One day Joe noticed a sign going up over a vacant lot in town. It read:

PROPOSED SITE OF ANOTHER HAMBURGER HOUSE.

Joe's heart sank. Hamburger

House was a vast business with hamburger places all over the country. Their restaurants were large and shiny, with white plastic counters and people in uniform working behind them. They produced hamburgers in two minutes, and these hamburgers, it was generally agreed, were fabulous.

Within a few days the builders started work on Hamburger House. Joe watched them lay the foundations, and then pour the concrete pillars into their moulds. At this rate, he thought, construction work would be finished in a couple of weeks. Once the painters had been and the equipment put in place, Hamburger House would be ready to challenge Mr Borthwick's.

That evening, Joe went down to Mr Borthwick's on his bicycle and

sat on one of the old stools that the old man kept in front of his counter. The place was deserted. Joe was the only person ordering a hamburger.

As Mr Borthwick prepared Joe's hamburger, Joe asked him what he felt about the new hamburger place.

"I've heard about it," Mr

Borthwick said. "I suppose that most people will go there when it opens."

"But what will you do?" Joe asked. "Will you close down?"

"I hope it won't come to that," Mr Borthwick replied, flipping Joe's hamburger onto a plate. "I've got nothing else to do. There's nowhere else to go."

Chapter 2

THE NEW HAMBURGER house opened its doors exactly one month later. The first day was a grand affair. To get as many people as possible to visit the shop, it was announced in the newspaper that on that day hamburgers would be served at half-price.

Of course this brought half the town out. At lunch time a long line of people stretched out of the shop and along the street, and again in the evening the place was packed with contented customers.

Hamburger House was opened by the mayor, who made a short speech and cut a piece of tape across the door. A giant hamburger was await-

ing him on the counter. There was a great popping of flash bulbs as the press men recorded this important event for the next day's newspapers.

Everyone agreed that the new place was excellent. There were shiny black and white tiles on the floor, a big white plastic counter, and a kitchen that sparkled with new equipment. While you waited for your order you could see the hamburgers sizzling away on the spotless cookers. Then, when your order was passed through to you, there were revolving sauce containers from which you could choose sauces of just about every colour.

Joe went along out of curiosity and had to admit the hamburger he chose was one of the best he'd ever tasted. Everyone else seemed to think so too, and as he walked out he heard somebody say to a friend, "You'd have to be crazy to go to Mr Borthwick's now."

Joe had rightly guessed that Mr Borthwick's days were numbered. Now, even fewer people went to his place. At night you could see a dimly lit Mr Borthwick sitting behind the counter waiting for somebody to come in for a hamburger. But nobody did.

Except Joe. Every now and then he would go down and order a hamburger. Mr Borthwick was always glad to see Joe, and took a lot of trouble with his hamburger. Then, when Joe had finished, he and Mr Borthwick would chat – about this and that and just about everything.

One evening, Mr Borthwick said to Joe, "Why not come into the kitchen and make your own hamburger? You can have this one free."

Joe was delighted. He went round to the side entrance and climbed up the wooden steps that led to the kitchen door. Mr Borthwick opened this for him and showed Joe round.

"Right," he said. "Now I'll show you how to make a hamburger."

Joe was fascinated. Mr Borthwick told him what to do and pointed out where things were kept. Then he let him get on with it.

Joe mixed the meat with a few chopped onions. Then he put the hamburger on the cooker and watched it sizzle. Mr Borthwick got out the two halves of roll and put these on a plate ready for the burger.

Joe was quite surprised when he found out that what he had made tasted like a hamburger at all.

"I've done it!" he exclaimed. "I've made a real hamburger."

Mr Borthwick beamed with pleasure. "Well done!" he said. "And now you've finished, you can make one for me."

Joe went down to Mr Borthwick's

two or three times a week and was always allowed to make his own hamburger. There were hardly any customers — a few people passing through town was the most that they could hope for. Then, one evening, just after he had made a hamburger for himself and one for Mr Borthwick, the old man suddenly whispered, "Look, we've got a customer."

Joe peered out of a corner of the service hatch and saw a man getting out of his car and coming up to the front door. He was a fat man dressed in a white suit and he was carrying a small brief case with him. Joe thought that he had seen him before, but he could not remember where.

Mr Borthwick went to the counter to serve him, but the man said that he did not want anything to eat.

"I've come to talk business," he said.

Joe strained his ears to hear what was being said but the man spoke too quietly. Now he remembered where he had seen this man before: he was the manager of Hamburger House and Joe had seen his photograph in the papers after the opening ceremony. Joe heard the door being closed and then Mr Borthwick came back into the kitchen and sat down.

"Well, well!" he said, wiping his brow. "What a nerve!"

Joe pretended that he had not been listening to the conversation so that Mr Borthwick would tell him all about it.

"They want me to sell out to them," the old man said. "They want to pension me off. And they want to do all this just so that they can get their hands on this place, make it all smart, and start charging fancy prices!"

"And do you think you'll ever sell?" Joe asked.

Mr Borthwick snorted angrily. "To that bunch? Never!"

Chapter 3

A FEW DAYS later when Joe went down to Mr Borthwick's he decided that he should make special burgers to cheer Mr Borthwick up, so he rummaged around amongst Mr Borthwick's old tins to find some seasoning to put into the meat.

There were three old tins which had herbs of some sort in them. They did not look as if they had been opened for years, but when Joe sniffed at the contents they seemed to be all right. Taking a pinch of this and a spoonful of that, Joe mixed the herbs with the beef and the onions. Then he put the two burgers on the cooker and watched them sizzle.

When the hamburgers were ready, Joe put Mr Borthwick's on a plate and handed it to him, and then helped himself to his own.

They had each taken a bite when they stopped and looked at one another.

"Joe!" shouted Mr Borthwick, his mouth still half-full of hamburger. "Joe! What have you done?"

What had Joe done? As he took his second bite, Joe realised the hamburger he had made tasted unlike any other hamburger he had ever had. It tasted so delicious and it smelled so exciting, that it seemed a pity even to think of eating it. Yet each bite invited another, and then after that another until soon both Joe and Mr Borthwick had finished altogether and had only their fingers to lick.

"That," said Mr Borthwick, "was

the best hamburger I've had in my life."

Joe knew that this sort of praise from an old hamburger-maker meant that the hamburger must have been every bit as good as he had thought it was. Now all that he had to do was to remember exactly how he had made it. He knew that he had taken the spices from three tins, but would he be able to remember how much of each he had put in?

Mr Borthwick lifted up one of the tins and sniffed at the spices inside. "I think I saw you putting in a spoonful of this," he said.

Joe looked doubtful. He thought he remembered putting in just a pinch of that spice, and two spoonfuls of one of the others. Still, he would try as Mr Borthwick suggested and put in a spoonful.

Soon two hamburgers were sizzling on the cooker. They certainly smelled good, but when Joe and Mr Borthwick tasted them, the taste that they were looking for was just not there. Disappointed, they put down the new hamburgers and tried again.

This time, Joe put in only a pinch of the first spice and slightly more of the others, but the result was still not what he wanted. He tried again, but still the hamburgers lacked that exquisite taste which had made the other burgers so beautiful.

Mr Borthwick shook his head.

"It's too late now," he said, looking at his watch. "We'll just have to try again some other time."

Joe could not get the memory of those magnificent hamburgers out of his mind. That night he dreamt that he had made them again, and in his sleep he tasted the marvellous taste of the perfect burgers. Unfortunately, the dream did not remind him of how he had made them, and so the next morning the mystery was still unsolved.

Joe wracked his brains trying to remember the recipe. He pictured the three spice tins. One was green and had a small picture of a tree on it. Another was brown and had been a biscuit tin before being used for spices. And the third, which was black, had nothing on it at all.

Joe remembered picking up the green tin and sniffing at the spice. Then he remembered putting it down and opening another tin. Now which tin was that? Was it the brown one that had been a biscuit tin, or was it the black one? "I think," said

Joe to himself, "it was the brown one."

Joe thought it was now beginning to come back to him.

"I picked up the brown tin," he whispered, "and then I put it down next to . . ." He hesitated before going on. "Yes, I put it down next to the black one. And then . . . and then I took just a little pinch from the black tin!" Joe felt a surge of excitement. He had now remembered one important thing. There was only a tiny bit of the contents of the black tin in those marvellous hamburgers.

"Now," Joe said. "The next thing I did was to pick up a spoon." It was all coming back to him. In his mind he had a clear picture of what had happened – surely he could make no mistakes now. "I picked up a spoon and took a spoonful from the . . . green tin!"

Joe gave a shout of delight. He had now worked out exactly what he had done. Still muttering to himself, he found a pencil and a piece of paper and wrote down the recipe. Then, without wasting any time, he rushed down to Mr Borthwick's with the good news of his discovery.

Mr Borthwick was as excited as Joe when he heard that Joe had remembered what he had done. Joe quickly mixed the meat and onions and then, under the watchful eye of Mr Borthwick, he took a pinch of spice from the brown tin and one from the black tin. Next, opening the lid of the green tin with the picture of the tree on it, Joe took out a spoonful.

Together they watched the hamburgers sizzling on the cooker. When they were done, Joe put them between the split halves of the rolls and passed one to Mr Borthwick. Neither of them dared bite into their burgers, so much seemed to be at stake.

Joe was the first to take a bite and the moment his teeth sank into the juicy burger he knew that his memory had not misled him. This was exactly the same taste as he had experienced the day before. It was so delicious that there could be absolutely no mistaking it.

Mr Borthwick agreed. "You've done it, Joe!" he shouted in triumph. "You've found the perfect hamburger!"

Joe was, of course, delighted that he had remembered his recipe. He had been worried that he would never be able to get the mixture just right, but now there seemed to be no doubt about it. He had the recipe – the exact recipe – for the finest hamburger in the world – the perfect hamburger.

When they had finished eating, Joe went across to the spice tins and examined them.

"Where did you get these from?" he asked Mr Borthwick.

The old man smiled. "Oh, they've been here almost since I opened this place. I hardly ever used them."

"What are the spices called?" he asked.

Mr Borthwick joined him at the table and picked up the black tin. Opening it, he took a sniff.

"That's sage," he said. It's pretty common. You get it in any supermarket."

Lifting up the brown tin, he examined the contents of that.

"And that," he said, "is rosemary. There's no mistaking that smell."

"Where do you get that from?" Joe asked.

"Any grocer," Mr Borthwick replied as he picked up the third tin, the green one with the picture of the tree on the front.

Mr Borthwick sniffed at the contents of the green tin and shook his head, puzzled. Tipping up the tin, he allowed a small amount of the spice to fall out onto the palm of his hand. This he examined, frowning and murmuring something under his breath.

"What is it?" Joe asked quickly. "What's it called?"

Mr Borthwick shook his head. "For the life of me, I just don't

know," he said. "I can't remember where on earth I got it."

Joe was now truly alarmed. "Doesn't the tin say anything?" he asked. "Can't we get some clue from that?"

Mr Borthwick looked the tin over. "Nothing at all," he said. "All that's there is a picture of a tree."

"But surely you can remember where you bought it," Joe pressed.

Mr Borthwick was flustered. He looked upset. "I'm sorry, Joe," he replied. "When you get to my age, your memory's not all that it might be. It can't be helped."

Joe felt a twinge of alarm. "If we don't know what it is, how are we going to get any more of it? There's only enough there for a few more burgers at the most."

Mr Borthwick nodded. "I know," he said softly.

Because he had been able to remember what he wanted to remember just by allowing his mind to mull over things, Joe thought that Mr Borthwick might be able to do the same. "By this time tomorrow he may have remembered," he said to himself.

But Mr Borthwick hadn't remembered the next day, nor the day after that.

"It's gone," he said sadly. "It's completely gone. I've got no idea at all about where I got that spice from."

Joe was not prepared to give up just because Mr Borthwick could not remember where the spice came from: perhaps they would be able to work it out some other way. He thought for a while, and then he made a suggestion.

"Who do you know," he asked, "who knows more about spice than anybody else?"

Mr Borthwick scratched his head. "Well," he said, "I think that the great Cassaroli probably knows more about spices and herbs than anybody else."

"Cassaroli?" Joe asked. "Who's he?"

Mr Borthwick smiled. "Cassaroli is probably the best Italian chef in the country. He works at the Excelsior Hotel and people come from miles around to taste his dishes. He's very famous."

"Do you know him?" Joe asked eagerly. "Can we go and see him?"

Mr Borthwick looked doubtful. "I've never actually met him," he admitted, "but I see no reason why we shouldn't go and see him. After all, you and I, we can speak to him chef to chef!"

Chapter 4

THE EXCELSIOR HOTEL was at a well-known resort about fifty miles away. When they reached the hotel, Mr Borthwick parked his car in the car park and together they walked round to the back of the building, where Mr Borthwick said they would find the kitchen entrance. There they were met by a porter, who asked them rather suspiciously what they wanted.

"We have come," Mr Borthwick said, "to see Mr Cassaroli."

The porter directed them along a passage and there, in front of them, was a wide door with a notice that said, "Kitchen. Entry forbidden."

Mr Borthwick straightened his tie and smoothed back his hair. Then, turning to wink at Joe, he pushed open the door and the two of them entered.

Joe had never seen such a magnificent kitchen. Stretching out in front of them were what seemed like acres and acres of tables and ovens. Extractor fans, like great hooded creatures, whirred busily, and steam rose from a dozen different pans. Here and there, standing in front of chopping boards or mixing bowls, men and women dressed all in white were preparing dishes. It was a remarkable sight.

As they entered, everyone suddenly stopped working and stared at them. Then, after a few moments, a short and extremely fat man clapped his hands angrily and everyone returned to work. The fat man waddled across towards Joe and Mr Borthwick and stood defiantly before them.

"How dare you enter my kitchen!" he shouted. "You must leave immediately!"

And with that he clapped his hands imperiously and began to waddle away.

"Excuse me," Mr Borthwick called out after the retreating figure.

"But I have come to see Mr Cassaroli."

The chef turned round. "I am the great Cassaroli," he said impatiently. "What do you want?"

Both Joe and Mr Borthwick were surprised. They had expected that anybody who called himself "the great Cassaroli" would look more impressive than this.

Mr Borthwick quickly overcame his surprise and began to explain what it was that he and Joe wanted. "We have heard," he began rather nervously, "that there is nobody who knows more about spices than you do."

As Mr Borthwick spoke these words, there was a marked change in Cassaroli's manner. The famous chef now relaxed a little and even allowed himself a modest smile.

"Yes," he said quite pleasantly. "That is said."

Mr Borthwick continued quickly. "And we wondered if you could identify a spice for us. We have it here." Joe passed Mr Borthwick the green tin and the old man gave it to the chef.

"Let me see, let me see," Cassaroli said impatiently, grabbing the tin from Mr Borthwick's hands. "This should not be difficult."

The chef opened the lid and poked his small fat nose in to sniff at the spice. He looked for a moment, frowned, and took another sniff. He took a small quantity of the spice out of the tin and examined it. Then saying something to himself in Italian, he put a little on his tongue to taste it.

"Mmm," he said, thoughtfully.

Mr Borthwick looked hopeful. "Can you recognize it?" he asked.

Cassaroli looked embarrassed. "I cannot," he said crossly. "It must be a very rare spice."

"But maestro," pleaded Mr Borthwick. "Surely you have tasted it somewhere before. You must have!"

Cassaroli shook his head regretfully and handed the tin back to Mr Borthwick. "I am sorry," he said. "But even the great Cassaroli has never tasted this spice."

Mr Borthwick and Joe must have looked so crestfallen at the news that even the great Cassaroli for a moment forgot his pride.

"There is one other possibility," he said quietly. "Eating in this hotel at this very moment is one of the world's great gourmets, a truly great

food expert. We will ask him. Perhaps he will tell us."

"Thank you," said Mr Borthwick. "You see, it is very important to us to be able to find more of this spice." Mr Borthwick didn't dare mention hamburgers, because he knew that to the great Cassaroli, hamburgers would be beneath contempt. Such a great chef had probably never even seen a hamburger.

Joe, Mr Borthwick, and the great Cassaroli left the kitchen and entered the grand dining room of the Excelsior. In front of them stretched table after table of starched white tablecloths and gleaming silver. In the middle of the room a vast candelabra of crystal glowed with a hundred points of light.

As the great Cassaroli entered the room, many of the diners looked up from their plates to stare at him. Then, at several tables at the same time, groups of diners rose to their feet and clapped their hands in enthusiastic applause. The chef stopped, bowed, and waved to those who had applauded. Then, together with his two companions, he made his way towards a table in the corner of the room where a tall man in a black suit and bow-tie was dining with a woman bedecked with glittering jewels.

As the famous gourmet saw Cassaroli approach, he rose to his feet and made a small bow towards the chef. Then he looked in the direction of Mr Borthwick and Joe and made a small bow towards them as well.

Cassaroli introduced them to the man and the woman. He was called Mr Octavius and his friend was called Miss Cadillac.

"We have come to ask your advice," Cassaroli said in an important voice.

Mr Octavius smiled modestly. "But my dear charming Cassaroli, who am *I* to advise *you*?" he said.

Cassaroli spread his hands. "For once I have failed," he said, sounding very upset about it all. "Where one has failed, another may succeed."

Mr Octavius listened to this gravely and then he turned his attention to Mr Borthwick's explanation about the mystery spice. Then, taking the tin and opening it carefully, he inspected the contents. Dipping a long and elegant hand into the tin, he took out a pinch of the spice and put it on the white tablecloth. From a pocket in his jacket he now extracted a small eye-glass, which he fixed over one eye.

Joe watched Mr Octavius inspecting the spice. After a minute or so, the gourmet put away the eye-glass and busied himself with placing a tiny bit of the spice on a small silver

spoon. Then he closed his eyes and put the spoon into his mouth.

Mr Octavius opened his eyes and gently withdrew the spoon from his mouth. "I think," he said slowly, "that I may be able to help you."

Joe was sure that Mr Borthwick's sigh of relief could be heard all over the vast dining room.

Mr Octavius raised one hand to

silence them. "I cannot be sure," he said, "in fact, I regret that I cannot give a name for this spice."

Of course everyone was disappointed and Cassaroli was about to protest when Mr Octavius continued.

"As you know well, Cassaroli," he said, "I have eaten all over the world. I have dined in France. I have dined up and down Italy, in restaurants in valleys and on the tops of mountains. I have sampled sweet cabbage in Poland and honey fingers in Greece. I have eaten my way across Australia and across South America – in both directions."

Joe listened with fascination as the famous gourmet continued. There was something quite masterly in the way he spoke, and Joe knew that he was in the presence of a great authority.

"And," said Mr Octavius, raising a finger into the air, "I have tasted some extremely unusual dishes. In Hong Kong I ate several snakes, all served in sauce. On the islands of China I ate ants, neatly spread on toast. They were delicious. And, of course, I have had so many helpings of bird's nest soup that I can hardly remember them all."

Cassaroli was entranced by this account. To a chef, such a man as Mr Octavius was worthy of the highest possible admiration.

"But enough of this!" said Mr Octavius. "To the business in hand!"

Joe hardly dared breathe. Would the famous gourmet give them the clue that would lead them to the spice?

"I *have* tasted this before," Mr Octavius announced, pointing to the green tin. "I tasted it many years ago. Since then I have never come across it."

"Where was it?" Mr Borthwick urged. "Can you remember?"

Mr Octavius lowered his voice, as

one does when one is about to reveal
a secret.

"I am ashamed," he whispered.

Cassaroli leaned forward. "Tell
us," he pressed. "We will tell
nobody."

Mr Octavius hesitated. "My only
excuse," he said, "was my hunger. I
hadn't eaten for eight hours, other-
wise I wouldn't have dreamt of going
there."

"Going where?" Cassaroli hissed.

Mr Octavius took a silk hand-
kerchief from his jacket pocket and
mopped at his brow. "It was late,"
he said. "Nobody else was open. I
was travelling through that town
down the road." He paused, looking
guiltily at Cassaroli. "Forgive me, it
was many, many years ago. I popped
into a hamburger shop!"

"A hamburger!" Cassaroli exclaimed. "You ate a common hamburger!"

"I shall never do it again," Mr Octavius pleaded. "But I must admit, it was a very fine hamburger indeed! I can't remember the name of the place. I think it was called Braithwaites or Bentinks – something like that . . . *Borthwick's*! That was it."

Chapter 5

"WE'RE BACK EXACTLY where we started," Mr Borthwick said as they drove home. "We're none the wiser."

Joe thought about this for a moment. It had been the most remarkable coincidence that Mr Octavius himself, the great gourmet, had, one evening long ago, slipped into Mr Borthwick's hamburger place. And it had been another coincidence that on that very evening Mr Borthwick had put a pinch of spice from the green tin into his hamburger.

"I hardly ever used that stuff," Mr Borthwick remarked. "I can't have been thinking what I was doing!"

But of course Mr Borthwick was right when he said that they were back where they began. A great chef and a great gourmet had both failed to identify the spice. They knew nothing more than they had known when they set out. It was most disappointing.

For the next few weeks nothing much happened at Mr Borthwick's hamburger place. Then, one evening when Joe called round to help Mr Borthwick paint some shelves, Mr Borthwick gave him some bad news.

"I don't think we'll bother to work tonight," he said dejectedly.

Joe was surprised. "But we were going to paint those shelves," he protested. "Why don't we start tonight?"

Mr Borthwick sat down on his

chair. He looked crumpled up, defeated.

"Listen to me, Joe," he said seriously. "We just can't go on. I owe the bank money. The business isn't profitable and now the bank manager says that if I don't pay up in three weeks then that will be that."

"Why has the bank suddenly decided to ask for their money back?" Joe asked.

Mr Borthwick looked up. "I think I know the reason," he said quietly. "One of their biggest customers is Hamburger House. The manager of Hamburger House and the manager of the bank have become close friends. Need I say more?"

A knot of anger gripped Joe's stomach. Mr Borthwick's enemies were determined to close him down at all costs.

Joe looked at the old man. The will to fight back seemed to have gone out of him altogether. If anyone is going to save the business, Joe thought, it will have to be me.

As he lay in bed that night, Joe thought of what he could do. To begin with, it all seemed so hopeless.

To pay the bank back, Mr Borthwick needed money, and he just did not have it. Unless he got it within three weeks, then he would have to sell up.

If Joe was going to save Mr Borthwick's business, he'd have to find somebody who would provide the money for Mr Borthwick to pay back the bank, or he would have to earn it himself. Joe did not know any wealthy people (nor did Mr Borthwick) so he decided their only hope lay in discovering the name of the mystery spice.

If only we had more of that wonderful magic spice, he thought, we could make hamburgers that would surprise the world. Nobody would go to Hamburger House if they could have one of our burgers instead! Somewhere, someone must know what the strange substance was.

Joe knew that Mr Borthwick must have bought the spice from somewhere, which meant that there might be a shopkeeper who would recognise it. If it had been bought as long ago as Mr Borthwick said it had, then the shopkeeper would be an old man. And, thought Joe, as long as he hasn't retired, I might be able to find him.

With all the enthusiasm of a detective on the trail, Joe went through the town directory, making a list of all the grocers. There were twenty in all, though some of them he knew were large supermarkets. These he struck off the list straight away. That left eleven. These Joe visited, one by one, speaking to each shopkeeper and showing him the green tin with the tree picture.

Two or three of the older ones were

helpful, but they couldn't say anything definite. Then, in a little shop
at the edge of town, Joe found an old
grocer who gave him his first clue.

"I *think* I *might* have seen a tin like
that," the old man said from behind
the counter. "It must have been a
long time ago."

Joe urged the old grocer to go on.

"Can you remember where you got it from?"

Joe's question was answered by a doubtful look. "I don't think so. It was an awfully long time ago."

The grocer thought for a while. "Just a moment," he said at last. "I happen to have some of my old catalogues — I keep them for memory's sake, you know."

The old man put the tin down on the counter and shuffled off into a back room. After a short while he returned, carrying a thick and rather tattered catalogue. In it there were photographs of shoes and bundles of string and funny old washing machines with big handles. The grocer flipped to the food section and began to turn over the pages very slowly.

"Dried vegetables," he muttered, "pickles, tinned Portugese sardines, red and green jelly squares, Danish caviar in small and large bottles . . ." He paused. "Spices."

Joe peered at the catalogue. The page where the old man had stopped was covered with columns of figures, but in between the figures were

tiny photographs of jars and tins. The grocer ran a finger down the columns, muttering something to himself.

Suddenly he stopped. "There," he said. "That's it! I knew I'd seen it!"

Joe felt like leaping onto the counter, he was so excited by the discovery.

"Where is it?" he cried. "Please show me."

"Well," said the grocer, "here's a picture of the tin – it *is* the same one, isn't it?"

Joe looked at the small photograph. Yes. There was no doubt that it was the tin. It was exactly the same shape and on the front a picture could be made out. It was a picture of a tree.

Underneath the picture of the tin, neatly printed in tiny lettering, were the words, "Mrs Bailey's Mixture. A taste-bud tickler for every occasion."

Joe read out this description and looked expectantly at the grocer. For a moment he looked puzzled but then, slowly but unmistakably, a smile of recognition spread over his face.

"Of course!" he said. "*Of course!*"

Joe was bursting to know what the grocer remembered, but he did not want to break the old man's train of thought.

"Well, well," the old man went on.

Joe counted to ten, then blurted out, "Who *is* Mrs Bailey?"

"Mrs Bailey?" came the answer. "She was a famous cook – used to be the best mixer of spices in the whole country. And she lived here, right in this town."

At this news, Joe's heart leapt. All that he had to do was find Mrs Bailey and then Mr Borthwick's troubles would surely be over.

"Where is she now?" he asked.

"Heaven, I expect," the grocer replied. "She died many years ago."

Joe felt the disappointment that

you feel when you get very close to something you want and then, at the last moment, find it snatched away from you.

"But her daughter still comes in here," the grocer added. "Every week, without fail. She looks just like her mother, but I hear that she can't tell one spice from another!" The grocer shook his head in disapproval.

To Joe that didn't matter. He was on the right track at last. Fortunately, the grocer was able to tell Joe where Mrs Bailey's daughter lived. Joe wrote down the address, thanked the grocer for his help, and set off to tell Mr Borthwick about the progress he had made.

Mr Borthwick had reconciled himself to the loss of his business and had already begun to pack away some of his old equipment. Now, as he heard

Joe's news, he seemed to get new courage for the fight.

"Once we get some more of the spice," Joe explained eagerly, "we can start to sell hamburgers that will make Hamburger House's hamburgers taste like wet cardboard. Everyone will come to us."

Mr Borthwick's eyes gleamed: it would be wonderful to have a thriving business once more.

"I'll expand!" he cried enthusiastically. "I'll buy new equipment!"

Joe was thrilled with the change in his friend's mood and he urged Mr Borthwick to launch an advertising campaign straight away.

"We must put advertisements in the newspapers," Joe said.

COMING SOON.

66

BORTHWICK'S TRADITIONAL HAMBURGERS. HAMBURGERS AS THEY *USED* TO TASTE!

Mr Borthwick nodded approvingly. "You're right, Joe. That's just what we will say. Everybody thinks things used to taste better. We'll show them that they really did!"

Together the two of them decided there should be a picture of Mr Borthwick standing over a hamburger, which would be cooking away on the cooker. Underneath would be written, in old-fashioned lettering:

Taste the secret recipe of the world's most famous old-fashioned hamburger! Try a Borthwick's Hamburger today!

67

So pleased were they with their plans that Joe and Mr Borthwick celebrated with an old-fashioned hamburger. Joe mixed the mixture, and as he did so, he used the very last bit of spice that the green tin contained.

Chapter 6

MR BORTHWICK AND Joe wasted no time in placing their advertisements: five days later, across the front page of the local papers, were the pictures of Mr Borthwick and the announcement of the impending arrival of the famous old-fashioned burgers.

"I thought Mr Borthwick was finished," Joe heard somebody say. "But he must have something up his sleeve after all."

"I haven't been there for months," another said. "Maybe I should give these new burgers a try when they arrive."

This was exactly what Joe and Mr Borthwick hoped people would say.

The only problem was that they had not yet found the supplies of the spice that they would need if their hamburgers were to be truly perfect. Joe realised (rather late) that it might have been better to wait before they put the advertisements in the newspaper. What if they failed to find the spice? Mr Borthwick would then look very foolish indeed.

Without wasting any more time, Joe and Mr Borthwick set off to find Mrs Bailey's daughter. It was a long street and they were almost at the top of it when they came to a gate on which the words OLIVE BAILEY had been painted in neat red letters.

Olive Bailey, a thin person who probably wasn't very interested in food, opened the door. "Come in," she said. "Why are you looking for me?"

For the next five minutes, Mr Borthwick talked non-stop, explaining to Olive Bailey why they were looking for her mother's spice and why it was so important that they get hold of some supplies of it as soon as possible. When he finished speaking, Olive Bailey sighed and shook her head.

"I'm sorry to disappoint you," she said sympathetically, "but my mother's kitchens were cleared out years ago. I've not even got any of the tins that she used to use. They all went."

Mr Borthwick looked down at the floor. Joe noticed that he had the same crumpled look as when he had first announced that the business would have to close. His body sagged. His face was grey.

"Please," Joe said to Olive Bailey.

"Please try to help us."

Olive Bailey smiled at Joe. "I was going to go on to say that there is something I might be able to do. I still have my mother's notebooks in the attic. I never got round to throwing them out. I think that some of them have recipes in them, but I'm not sure."

Both Joe and Mr Borthwick jumped to their feet at the same time.

"We should be grateful if you'd let us see them," Mr Borthwick said.

"We'd take great care of them," Joe added.

Olive Bailey left the two of them for a few minutes to return, looking rather dusty, with several old notebooks.

"Here," she said, handing the books to Mr Borthwick. "With any

luck you will find what you need in there."

Joe could not wait until they got back to Mr Borthwick's to look into the notebooks. As they drove back, he thumbed through the thick books. Inside, written in a rather spidery handwriting, was recipe after recipe. Take two pinches of this and three spoons of that: take three apples and cut them into squares: take two potatoes and put them in a pot: and so on.

"There are thousands and thousands of recipes here," Joe complained.

"Just look for one which has 'spice' written at the top," suggested Mr Borthwick. "That's the one we're after."

"But I can't," Joe said sadly. "None of them has anything written at the top!"

There was only one thing that Joe and Mr Borthwick could do. They would have to go through all the recipes, one by one, choosing those that looked as if they might be for the spice. Then, having done this, they would have to test each of them in turn.

"If only she'd labelled her recipes," Joe wailed as he and Mr Borthwick measured out ingredients for the fortieth time. "It would have been so much easier for us right now!"

Slowly they worked through the notebooks. As they neared the end, Joe began to despair. As they tried out the last recipe, he *knew* that they would fail. He hardly had the energy to measure out the ingredients and Mr Borthwick barely bothered to taste the mixture that they had made.

"Any good?" Joe asked as Mr Borthwick put his tongue into the mixture on the spoon.

For a few seconds Mr Borthwick said nothing, and then he merely shook his head. "Taste it yourself," he said.

Joe took a little of the mixture and dabbed it on the tip of his tongue. No. That was not it. It was far too peppery.

"That's it, Joe," Mr Borthwick said wearily. "There's only one thing to do."

"What's that?" Joe asked, dreading the answer.

"I'm going to place an advertisement in the newspaper saying that we will definitely be closing next week. I shall thank all my old customers and leave it at that."

He looked round at the familiar cookers and the tatty stools that he had known for so many years. Then he stepped out of the door and was gone.

Joe sat alone in the kitchen. He had done all he could to help Mr Borthwick, but it had not been enough. Hamburger House had won, and that was all there was to it.

Idly, he picked up one of Mrs Bailey's notebooks and flicked through the well-thumbed bulk of recipes. They had tried all the likely ones and none of them had proved to be the right one. Joe looked at the back cover. It was very dirty as it had picked up a lot of stains from spending its life in a kitchen. Underneath the grime there was some sort of picture. Joe struggled to make out what it was.

For a few moments he hardly dared believe what he saw. Could it really be that? Joe held the book up to the light and at that moment all his hopes were realised.

There, on the grimy cover of the book, so covered with stains that they had not noticed it, was a picture of a tree. And there was no mistaking it – it was the same tree that appeared on the tins of spice. Beneath it could just be made out a list of ingredients. It was the recipe for Mrs Bailey's Mixture.

As Mr Borthwick was handing over the advertisement which was to appear in the next day's papers, the newspaper clerk answered the telephone. "Yes," he said. "He's right here."

Mr Borthwick was surprised to hear Joe at the other end of the line. Quietly he listened to Joe's message and then he handed the receiver back to the clerk.

"I want to change this advertisement," he said firmly. "I want it to read:

To be launched tomorrow – Borthwick's Old-Fashioned Hamburger. At last – the perfect hamburger!"

The clerk wrote down the wording of the advertisement and Mr Borthwick rushed back to his hamburger place where Joe was waiting for him.

On the day that the perfect hamburger was launched word spread quickly that something important was happening at Mr Borthwick's. For the first time in months there were queues of people waiting to be served, and all the tatty stools were occupied. Everyone who bought a burger agreed: they *had* tasted the perfect hamburger. Some people had two, and one rather greedy customer ate six.

The newspapers sent reporters to interview Mr Borthwick's customers and not a single one had anything but praise for the old-fashioned hamburgers.

"How would you describe the taste?" one reporter asked a satisfied customer.

"I'd describe it as ... Well, it's like ... No, that's not quite like it ... It's just like ... Oh, taste it yourself!"

Joe was delighted at the way things turned out. Now that Mr Borthwick had so many customers, he was able to buy new equipment, have the walls painted and the stools recovered. Nobody went to Hamburger House any more, and it was Hamburger House which now stood empty at night.

But Joe and Mr Borthwick had their greatest satisfaction one evening when a car drew up outside their hamburger place and out stepped three people they had met before. There, on the pavement, stood none other than the great Cassaroli and, elegant and beaming, Mr Octavius and Miss Cadillac.

The three special visitors ordered a large hamburger each, which Joe and Mr Borthwick prepared with extra care. Then, after they had finished eating, they agreed to join Joe and Mr Borthwick in the kitchen for a celebration.

"I have a small gift for you," the great Cassaroli said. "Here it is."

Mr Borthwick pushed Joe forward to receive the gift from the hands of the great chef. It was a beautiful silver spoon, and on it had been inscribed the words: *To the makers of the perfect hamburger – from the great Cassaroli.*

Mr Borthwick was so pleased with this great compliment that he had to wipe away a tear of joy that had begun to run down his cheek.

"Maestro," he said. "How can we thank you enough?"

"That's simple," snapped the great Cassaroli, "make me another hamburger!"

A weekend of chaos in a snappy little tale

Slap bang in the middle of the coldest day of the year the heating has broken down and all the animals are freezing (apart from the polar bear). So, Mr Pickles, the zoo director, asks each keeper to take their animal home for the weekend to keep them warm.

What could possibly go wrong?

Magical adventures in a bestselling series

Mr Majeika

When Mr Majeika is in charge, there are bound to be tricks in store for Class Three.

Mr Majeika – he's a wizard in the classroom.

Where there's trouble, there's bound to be

Bad Becky

but you can't help loving her!

After all, wouldn't you prefer to hear a story
about a princess-gobbling dragon than
some soppy fairy tale?

Very good stories about a BAD little girl!

The furry bundle has arrived.

'Okay, okay. So hang me. I killed a bird.
For pity's sake, I'm a cat.'

Get your claws out for the hilarious antics of Tuffy
and his family as told by the killer cat himself.
If you know cats, you'll understand.

'A brilliant tale of catastrophe and pussy pandemonium'
– *Daily Telegraph*

annefine.co.uk   myhomelibrary.co.uk

Inside every boy there's a hero . . .
and Luke Lancelot is the
bravest knight of all.

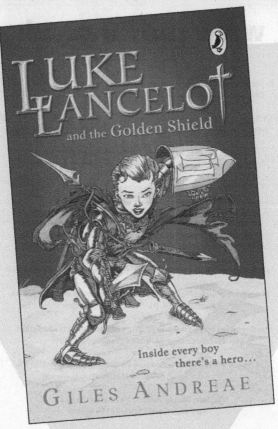

But an action-packed adventure of
fire-breathing dragons, death-defying duels
and hidden dangers is enough to put even
the boldest knight's bravery to the test.

Read more in Puffin

For complete information about books available from Puffin – and Penguin – and how to order them, contact us at the appropriate address below. Please note that for copyright reasons the selection of books varies from country to country.

www.puffin.co.uk

In the United Kingdom: Please write to Dept EP, Penguin Books Ltd, Bath Road, Harmondsworth, West Drayton, Middlesex UB7 0DA

In the United States: Please write to Penguin Group (USA), Inc., P.O. Box 12289, Dept B, Newark, New Jersey 07101–5289 or call 1–800–788–6262

In Canada: Please write to Penguin Books Canada Ltd, 10 Alcorn Avenue, Suite 300, Toronto, Ontario M4V 3B2

In Australia: Please write to Penguin Books Australia Ltd, 250 Camberwell Road, Camberwell, Victoria 3124

In New Zealand: Please write to Penguin Group (NZ), Private Bag 102902, North Shore Mail Centre, Auckland 10

In India: Please write to Penguin Books India Pvt Ltd, 11 Panscheel Shopping Centre, Panscheel Park, New Delhi 110 017

In the Netherlands: Please write to Penguin Books Netherlands bv, Postbus 3507, NL–1001 AH Amsterdam

In Germany: Please write to Penguin Books Deutschland GmbH, Metzlerstrasse 26, 60594 Frankfurt am Main

In Spain: Please write to Penguin Books S. A., Bravo Murillo 19, 1° B, 28015 Madrid

In Italy: Please write to Penguin Italia s.r.l., Via Felice Casati 20, I–20124 Milano

In France: Please write to Penguin France S. A., 17 rue Lejeune, F–31000 Toulouse

In Japan: Please write to Penguin Books Japan, Ishikiribashi Building, 2–5–4, Suido, Bunkyo-ku, Tokyo 112

In South Africa: Please write to Longman Penguin Southern Africa (Pty) Ltd, Private Bag X08, Bertsham 2013